Nathaniel's 1st Day of School

A Story with a Twist

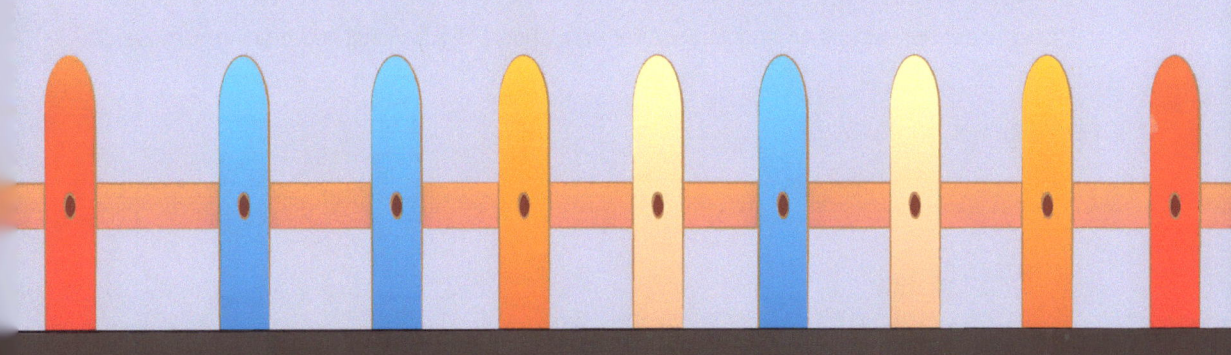

By Krysta Williams and Nathaniel Dawkins

Nathaniel's 1st Day of School

Publisher

Vike Springs Publishing Ltd.

London – United Kingdom

www.vikesprings.com

First Edition

ISBN-13: 978-1-7390951-1-6 Ebook

ISBN-13: 978-1-7390951-2-3 Paperback

ISBN-13: 978-1-7390951-3-0 Hardback

Printed in the

United Kingdom and the United States of America

For further information or to contact Krysta and publisher's please send an email to: krystawilliams.theauthor@gmail.com and admin@vikesprings.com respectively. Krysta and Nathaniel's books are available at special discounts when purchased in bulk for children's organisations, groups or as donations for educational, inspirational and training purposes.

LIMITED LIABILITY/DISCLAIMER OF WARRANTY

DEDICATION

This book is dedicated to my son. I love him very much and want him to grow and develop to be his best self. We really enjoyed writing this book together.

To God be the glory, great things he has done! Galatians 1:5 and Psalm 126:3

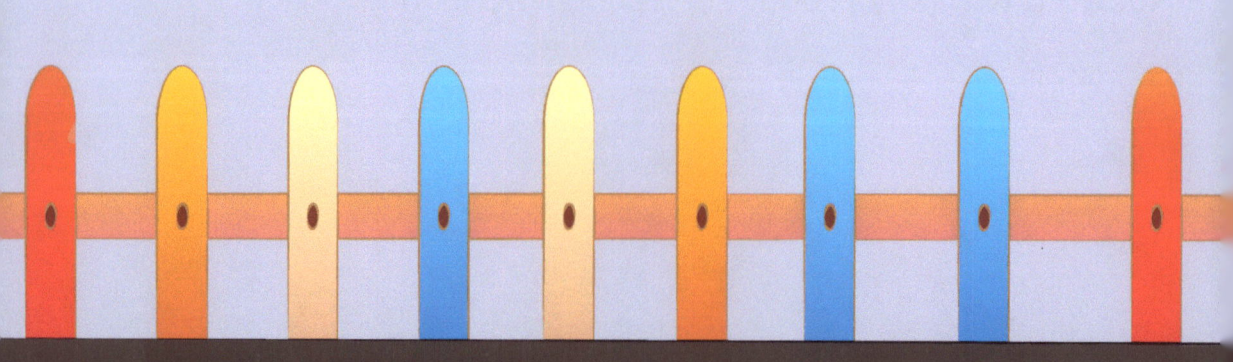

INTRODUCTION

Nathaniel is a four-year-old boy, who is **extremely nervous** about his first day of school. He **conquers** his **fears** with some help from his mother. Through her **special motivation,** she is able to **remodel** his thinking and **calm his nerves**. His mom has the **remedy** to **address** all of his **worries**, while giving him **reminders** of the **golden rules**. By the end of their talk, he is ready for his first day of school with an **eagerness** to learn, play and meet new friends. He now **understands** that school is a **safe, exciting** and **happy** place. Nathaniel is **eager** and ready to begin his new **journey**.

Note: please refer to the glossary that is located at the back of the book for the definitions of the words highlighted in **BOLD**. The glossary also defines other words that are used throughout the story.

It was the first Monday of September. Nathaniel's first day of school.

The beginning was here. The classroom was ready for the excited new children, like Freddie. The teacher was eager to meet them; so, she was there, waiting to greet them.

She opened the door. BOOM! The classroom was flooded with precious little children. ZOOM!

The smiles on their faces showed the hope in their hearts to meet lots of new friends and learn to be smart.

"Nathaniel, are you ready for your first day of school?" Nathaniel's mother asked, as she walked him to class.

"NOOOO!", Nathaniel cried; his face looked spaced and his head moved fast from left to right in haste...

It seemed, Nathaniel wasn't ready at all. He felt scared and confused, he wasn't having a ball.

"I'm a bit nervous!", he said, as he felt a bit small.

Nathaniel then asked, "do I HAVE to learn this fall?"

His mom replied, "learning is a specialty to take you where you want to be, from ABC to 123. Learning will be fun for you and me."

Nathaniel's mom gave him advice, without thinking twice. Isn't that nice?

Learning is fun so you don't have to run. For the time has come and it must be done.

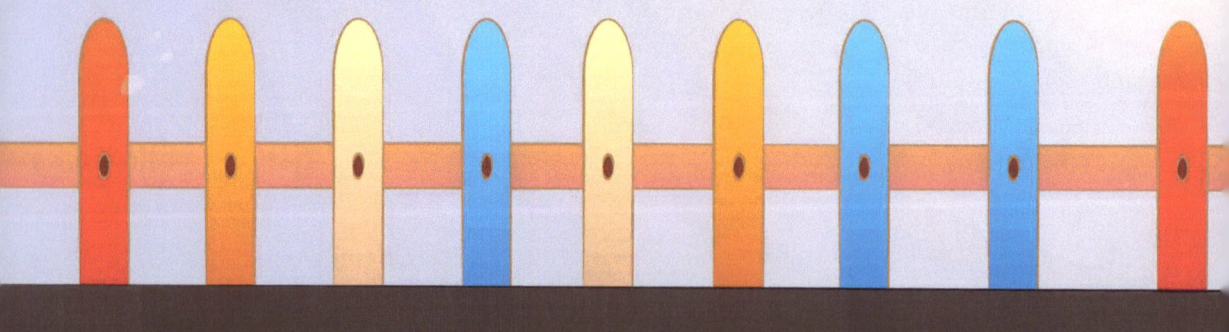

He wondered, "but what about friends? They are hard to find. I would like to make new ones who could be called mine."

Nathaniel expressed what his heart desired and his mom responded in the way required.

"Making new friends can sometimes be a test, but once you do they will be the best. So be caring and be kind because friendships are better when you show the behaviour that is similar to the kind of friends you would like to find."

Nathaniel then noticed his teacher by the door and thought to inquire, as he needed to know more. "Will my teacher be nice?" He pondered, then wondered some more.

His mom read his mind and answered in time. To conquer his doubts, she told him this rhyme:

"Teachers are wonderful, caring and kind. While you are at school, they will guide and develop your mind. For when they teach, you will learn and discover the world. And the treasures you will find are the answers to the questions from learning of all kinds."

She was doing her best to prepare him for school. So, she next gave him examples of the golden rules.

"Always put your hand up before you ask a question, or when you want to go to the toilet. Please wash your hands before and after you use it."

"Always wait your turn. You must not jump the queue."

"Always remember your manners. Say, please, excuse me, and thank you."

"Always try your best; God will do the rest."

"So be a good boy; practise the rules, and always remember that Mommy loves you."

"But mom, will I ever get to play outside?" Nathaniel exclaimed, like he wanted to cry.

"Outside activities are definitely a must, when the time is right, you'll get to do this without a fuss. So, until then, just sit, listen and learn. When you pay attention there will be so much to earn."

After addressing Nathaniel's concerns, his mom kissed his forehead and released a sigh. She then promised to return, as it was time to say goodbye. She quickly turned for the exit, because she didn't want to cry.

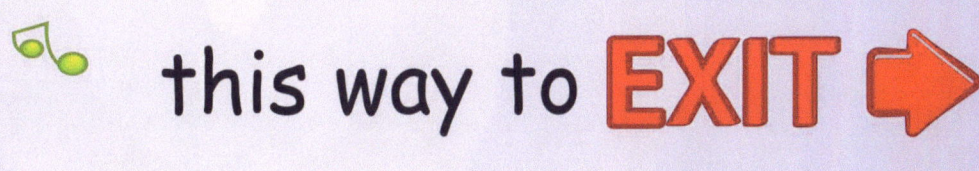

this way to EXIT

Nathaniel took his seat and got ready to strive.

He learnt the alphabet, numbers and text. It was so much fun; he was no longer vexed.

He met lots of new friends: Sally and Bill were the best! They taught him to paint; he taught them to share. For sharing is caring. You must always be fair.

His teacher, Mrs. Love, was as awesome as can be. She was the image of her name; so loving and so kind. It made him realise that school would be fine.

Before he knew it, it was nap time. So, he rested and dreamt of play time.

Nap Time.......Silent Area

Now it was outdoor play, his favourite pastime.

Outside on the playground; what more could he find?
His love for the playground was one of a kind.

From the swings and then to the slide. But just as it was Nathaniel's turn to go down the slide, he heard a voice say...

Nathaniel's Room

"Nathaniel, are you ready for your first day of school?"

His eyes opened quickly then he realized that he was still in his bed with his mom by his side.

What a surprise!

He jumped out of bed with a smile on his face and an eagerness to get ready, as he should not be late.

Nathaniel's Room

"Mom, is it time for my first day of school?" Nathaniel asked.
"Today is going to be a great day!" he gasped. "I will be fine."

GLOSSARY

Activities- things that people spend time doing.

Address- to speak to someone / it can also be someone's home address.

Advice- an idea offered as help in making a choice.

Alphabet- the letters of a language, given in proper order.

Awesome- causing awe (a feeling of wonder mixed with respect or fear).

Behaviour- the way a person acts or behaves, mostly when relating to others.

Boom - a deep or loud noise / a time of great success or favorable outcomes.

Care- a feeling of worry or to show serious attention.

Confuse- to not understand.

Conquer- achieve and overcome by strength of mind or character.

Definitely- without a doubt, certainly, surely, unquestionably.

Desire- to want or wish for.

Develop- to make someone or something better.

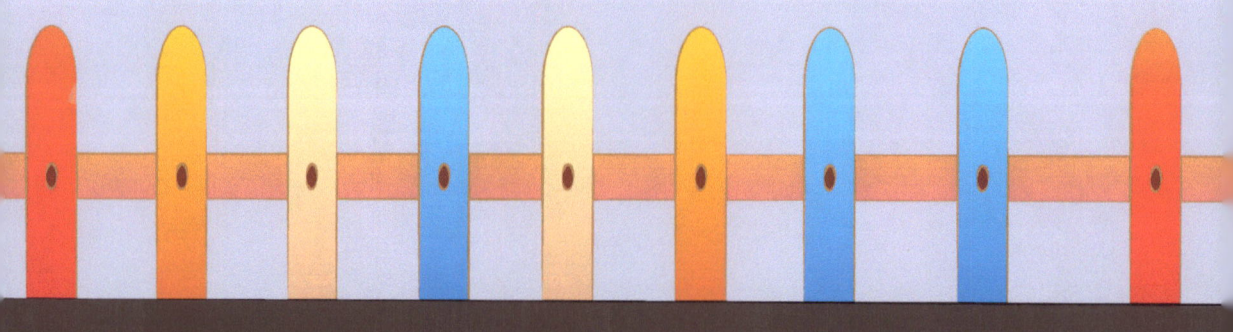

Discover- to find, locate or come across.

Doubt- to not know for sure.

Eager(ness)- wanting very much.

Earn- to get or deserve because of hard work or behaviour.

Examples- guide, sample, or a listed few.

Exciting- causing great feeling of eagerness.

Expressed- to make your feelings known.

Extremely- very, most or to a great extent.

Fair – to be good or honest.

Fall- the season of autumn / stumble, trip, drop or drop down, come down or go down.

Favourite- liked over all others.

Fear- to be scared of something or someone that is believed to be bad (dangerous).

Find- to learn or discover something, mostly something new.

Fine- very good.

Flooded- to be filled with / to enter in very great amounts or quantities.

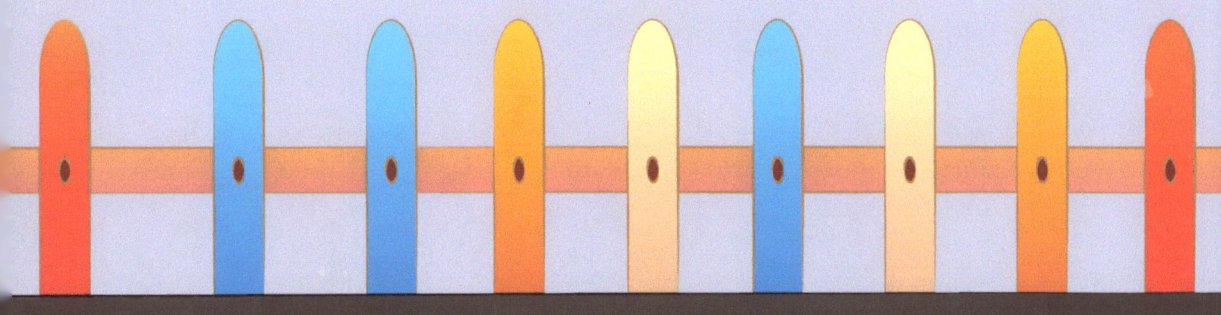

Friendship- being a friend.

Fuss- the show of unnecessary or excessive concern about something.

Golden Rules- rules to live by, something that should always be done.

Glossary- a brief dictionary related to a specific subject or text.

Greet – to say hello, give a polite word or sign of welcome.

Guide- to lead along the way for something that is not familiar.

Happy- content, cheerful, cheery, merry, joyful, jovial, jolly. Jumping for joy.

Hard- not easy, difficult / solid, firm, not easily broken, bent, or pierced.

Having a ball- enjoying one's self.

Haste- speed or hurry.

Image- a picture in your head.

Journey- to go on a trip from one place to another.

Jump- to hop on one's legs and feet / to move in front of someone who is waiting before you.

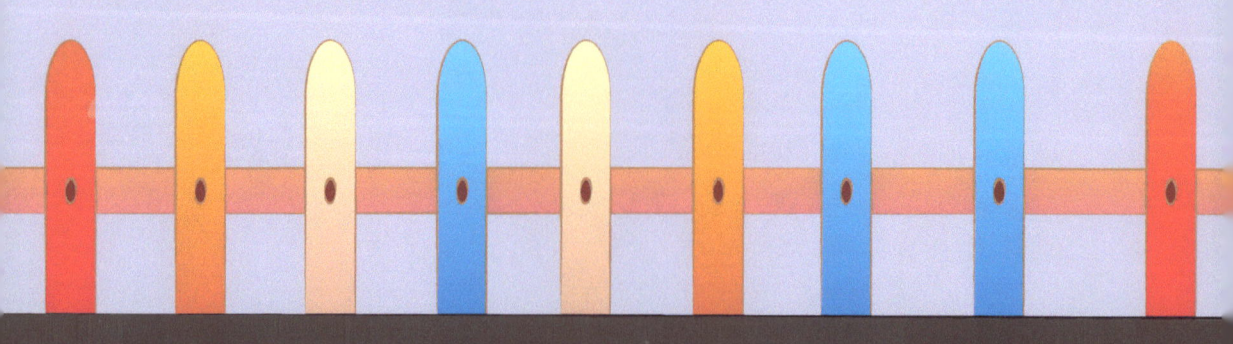

Kind- to be friendly / different types or category.

Late- not on time.

Learn- to find out about something new.

Meet – come face to face with someone, to come across or make contact with someone.

Mind- the part of a person that thinks, understands, remembers and feels.

Mine- something belonging to me.

Motivation- the reason for a person's behaviour or action.

Nervous- being fearful of a situation.

Noticed- to become aware of.

Outside- any space not indoors.

Pastime- an activity that makes time pass in a nice way.

Pay Attention- to look, listen and observe.

Pondered- to think about something deeply and carefully.

Precious- someone or something that is of great value.

Queue- a line of people or vehicles waiting their turn.

Quick- fast.

Realise- to become aware of or to understand.

Release- to let go of.

Remedy- cure or to make better.

Reminder- make something known to someone more than once or to repeat.

Remodel- to change.

Require- to need.

Respond- to answer.

Rhyme- a word that ends with the same or almost the same sound as another word.

Safe- not likely to be harmed or lost, protected from or not exposed to danger.

Scared- to be frightened or afraid. Worried or nervous.

Sigh- to breathe out with a long breath because of being sad, tired, or relieved.

Similar- the same, alike, close to, almost identical.

Share- to give or enjoy together with others.

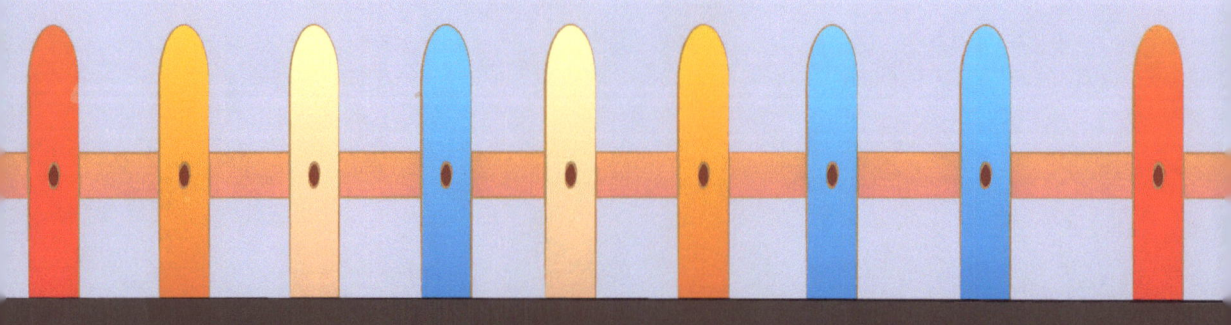

Small- little / to not believe in one's self (low confidence).

Smart- clever, intelligent, wise.

Spaced- showing lack of thought or emotion.

Special- better, greater or otherwise more than the usual, unusual or outstanding.

Specialty- a special skill.

Strive- to try or work hard.

Surprise- something that happens that is not expected.

Taught- past tense of teach.

Teach- to show or help to gain knowledge.

Teacher- a person whose job is to teach.

Test- trial, to try out, carry out trials on / to find out how much someone knows, their ability to do something.

Text- the words that appear in anything written or printed.

There- over there, position or direction.

Their- it belongs to them.

Thought- the act of thinking.

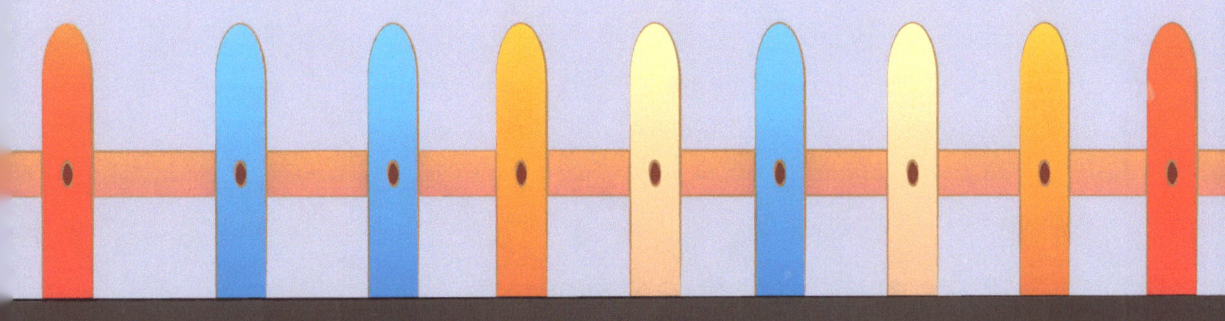

Treasures- something of great value.

Understand- to know or become aware of something.

Vex- to worry.

Wondered- to want to know or be curious about.

Wonderful- causing feelings of wonder; excellent or amazing.

Worries- when the mind overthinks on a matter that is important to someone.

Zoom- to move quickly, suddenly or sharply.

ACKNOWLEDGEMENTS

I would like to thank my family and friends for their role in the writing of this book. Your listening ears and opinions were greatly appreciated. My mother, husband, brothers and friends are the best.

My son and I would like to thank Victor Kwegyir and his team for their hard work and contributions in making this book the best that it could be. Thank you for making our dream a reality.

www.ingramcontent.com/pod-product-compliance
Lightning Source LLC
Chambersburg PA
CBHW041004170626

46815CB00002B/156